For Dreas

First published 1983 by
Walker Books Ltd,
17-19 Hanway House,
Hanway Place, London W1P 9DL

© 1983 Helen Oxenbury

First printed 1983
Printed and bound by
L.E.G.O., Vicenza, Italy

British Library Cataloguing in Publication Data
Oxenbury, Helen
The dancing class. – (First picture books)
I. Title
823'.914 [J]   PZ7

ISBN 0-7445-0036-2

The Dancing Class

Helen Oxenbury

WALKER BOOKS
LONDON

Mum said I should go
to dancing classes.

'We'll take these tights. She'll
soon grow into them.'

'We'll just make your hair
tidy like the others'.'

'Heads up, tummies in,
knees straight and point
your toes,' the teacher said.

'Don't cry, you'll soon learn.
I'll show you the right way
to tie up your shoes.'

'You danced very well,' the teacher told me. 'Will you come again next week?'

'This is what we do, Mum.
Watch. I'll do the gallop
all the way home.'